Pink

Grapefruit

Poetry & short love stories

Ry Reed

Books by Ry Reed

A H.E.R.O.S PROJECT series

A H.E.R.O.S PROJECT 12

Poetry

Pink Grapefruit

White Orchids

The little red poetry book called heartbreak

Grey Storm Clouds

I love my parents.

I want to begin with that.

They are not perfect, but I know they love me. I was inspired to write this book because

I witnessed it all: what an unhealthy relationship looks and breathes and walks like. Homely monsters embodied in two souls. My parent's dysfunction was my fall, because, I could not escape it. Late night arguments grew violent, doors were slammed, cups were thrown, threats were made, shouting competitions left me drowning on either side. You start off wielding a beaten white flag, sorting through anger and resentment, but anger is a contagious thing. It spreads from victim to victim and you find yourself hating the place you call home, remembering it's where you first learned *love*. It wasn't until, many years later, I tallied up all my failed relationships, wondered why I was so sensitive to loud noises, don't rely on those who unconditionally love me, how I thought I was the reason for my parents' misfortunes, and, not once, but three times, I tried committing suicide… I learned something… *I am in control of my heart.* I am in control of my surroundings. I am allowed to love those worthy of my special blend of tenderness. After my last suicide attempt, I vowed to never pity myself again and took up writing, firstly, as a habit to ease my sore wounds but my habit spun to love, and I wrote what I loved. To my surprise, my fractured heart slowly puzzled together, and barren white pages taught me how to construct a new one. A stronger, more durable heart. My mission fogged clear amidst my recovery: to share what knowledge lives hidden in my bones.

To you, my reader, thank you.

Love is not difficult, loving difficult people is.

-Ry Reed

CONTENTS

11

PART ONE

SUMMER

Love can be very addicting

You'll do whatever it takes to get another fix

Compromise your character to fit a mold

Then once it's all over,

You don't recognize the person standing in the mirror.

Love overdose

Actions really do speak louder than words.

Words have a way of cutting spirit and soul

Make you believe lies about yourself.

Sticks and Stones

When he decided to leave, I learned to stop chasing him

My feet grew too sore

The race was too repetitive

Tired

Fathers,

Your love is the first she will witness

Above her cradle

Aside from breast and chest

She will be drawn to your protection

Emulate it in every man of her choosing

So, let your love be gentle and kind and sweet

She'll replicate your recipe with accurate precision

And bake a love worth feeding her own.

My father's recipe

Understand

She isn't angry,

But bitter

Because

She's been through more heartache and disappoints

Than any woman will ever deserve.

That's why she stopped waiting up for you at night

A bitter end

Roses were his go to gift

After he made her cry a thousand storms over

She would water them soundly

And tire of floating on lonely oceans

That never warmed her up like

Apologetic embrace

It's a shame

Peace offering

Staying in an unhealthy relationship is like standing in the sunlight

In the beginning

The sun warms your skin and cheeks

Will inspire you to play in high and low grassy fields

Where crickets kiss feet

You feel as light as a sheet

The true threat goes unnoticed

No alarm is rung to uncover it

You won't see it unless

Old wounds can detect deadly concerns

Sunburns are like that

They burn, unknowingly

Sunblock

He came bearing flowers

Daisy's

Your favorite.

You convinced yourself

They were your favorite

His words are smoother than silk

Rehearsed to replicate tender caress upon neck to breast

He begged

And begged

Flashed rings and gold things

Anything to entice you

His mission was intent

He wanted inside

You were the gatekeeper

He affectionally won over

Gatekeeper

When he says

What he wants you to believe

Ask him the same question

A week from that very day

To see if his answer is consistent.

Lying is a hard costume to upkeep

After a while

If the act grows tiresome

He'll discard his mask

For his normal attire

Dr. Jekyll and Mr. Hyde

It's like leading a lamb to the slaughterhouse

Seek out the purest she-kind

When she has wandered from

Shepherds protective sight

Lure with delights

Her young heart imagines

Trail her far

Far

Far

Away from all she has ever known

So none can rescue her

When she cries out for help

Lonely lamb

Kisses have the magical effect

Of making you forget

The night before

Magic

Yelling and talking are two different forms of communication

Yelling is the toxic form

Just in case you didn't know

Just in case

I would rather live alone

Than feel lonely

In a relationship

Choice

Hugs can be given as a prescription drug.

But there is no cure for misery.

Prescription drugs

She told him she hated him

He told her he hated her

They stopped holding hands

They stopped spending romantic evenings in the park together

They stopped confiding in each other

They stopped being civil in front of the kids

They stopped caring to say I love you after a long day

But

They stayed together in the same bottomless pit

Refusing to ever climb out

A hopeless situation

Gifts are cover up offerings

Sent to the tattered and bruised

Effect infiltrating

Familiar grounds

Bent on stealing peace

Tactics of war

Don't bargain your love

For anything less than

Gold.

Plastic isn't worth much.

Conned

What is love

But a tug and a pull on

To and cords

That sway hips

And buttocks to a rhythm know of their own

Sung on romantic mid-night strolls

In the confines of secrets and lengthy promises

Locked with a smooch

Sealed tightly by time and hard circumstances

Jitterbug

It truly is quiet right before a storm

When storms come

They destroy everything in their wake

Leave you deserted and wandering

In foreign terrains

Until a life vest is thrown

Sole survivor

Long breaks clear the mind

And bridge back

Scattered pieces

Lost along the way

Missing pieces

Love lessons can be taught

To those with patient hearts

And understanding attitude

But not everyone is patient enough to learn

A woman's pains

Because she is a complicated book

With many chapters and uppercased words

Skipping pages

Folding corners

Miss placing her long awaited memoir

Tells her you don't care

To read the lines etched

Between her story and bones

The story of my life

She only smiled when it was necessary

To please those she loved and adored

Crying

Tossing relentlessly at night

Was done in private

Pretty girls smile

There is nothing colder than a woman's scorn

It creeps into every bit of food

Until even the sweetest fruits

Are sour

Sour grapes

Her world was neither pink or blue.

She slept under grey clouds.

Today's forecast

She stressed

She fretted

She worried

She complained

She cursed

She screamed

She slept

She started a new day just the same

Rinse and repeat

Underlining brown eyes

Slumber problems

That not even she knows how to resolve

Cause her to stare at the moon

And wish

For change to come sooner

Dark under circles

His love shouldn't hurt the way it does.

The reality

fs

I've come to accept two things:

1. Love isn't for the weak and only the strong may prevail.
2. Love can make you weak if the dishonest prevail.

Thing one and thing two

Summer had just begun….

She was young, and questioned his love, though, her gut told her no and she wasn't sure what to do with the seed of life growing inside her womb. She had heard stories, seen him day to day, thought and wondered, *what if*? She had been alone and discarded. No man had learned to appreciate the fine silk weaves she taught herself to sow. She could spin leftover cotton to suede fittings and tattered scraps into beautiful red dressings even God himself awed with amazement and pride. But, she did not value such crafted hands or such rose colored hair or her gift of tongue, and she married. To her regret, because his love was colder than that carat of ice he twisted on her small finger.

Married too young

She loved him enough to take him back, even when he didn't deserve an ounce of her forgiveness. Her love was too forgiving.

Forgiveness

Hand holding

Is the most subtle

Form

Of

Body language

Dance of hands

There's something about love

That keeps you up

All night

Way past your bedtime

Though

You have to wake up early

For work

And one hour of sleep

Isn't ever enough

Phone calls

I've stared deep into your eyes

And found a soul worth

Fishing for

I just hope

My bait is

Sweet enough

Catfishing

If you love me, tell me so

Why play games

Keep me questioning

The time I spent

Telling you my every secret

Chess

You'll know it's real

When

He finally has the guts

To

Check

Taken

On Facebook

The stone ages

When she looked at him

She never saw any of his mistakes

It was an illusion of possibilities

What if he changes?

That kept her invested

Houdini

Listen to a classic love song

When you're in a serious relationship

Does it sound different now?

Do the lyrics finally make sense?

I recommend Fire and Desire

By Rick James and Teena Marie

Fiery passion

Stars

In many ways

Are like scars

Every twinkling sketch

Distracts your eyes from the canvas beneath

To where

You can no longer

Marvel

A beauty so profound and quiet in nature

It encompasses every reach

Baring only

Alluring imagination

For a good man to construct

A good astronomer

I have sailed to the same *place*

Where your mind and heart

Rest

In order

To say hello

Before anyone else

Good morning

Summer afternoons are best spent

Under leaf tree limbs

Lounged and tangled about on a worn red blanket

The shade is cool enough

That ice in lemonade melts slowly

Vagabond clouds

Offer animal shapes and laughs

To hold you over

Until

A pink sunset whispers good luck

Promising an even better night

Picnic

Some promises are made

Too early on

And neither lover

Knows who

They are swearing to

Promise ring

You've got it bad

When you stare at your phone all day

And hope he/she texts you

When you know

You're not supposed to be on

Your phone at work

Nine to five

She sadly never understood

Her value

She offered her every pearl

To curious fishermen

Lost at sea and heavy with youthful pride

Today

Nothing graces her collarbone

For the man

Who she had been longing for

Lost at sea

She was his sun

That cast creeping downpour away

The warmth upon cheek

The heat beneath sand and rock and grain.

He closed his tired eyes

While listening to June ocean waves

That cooled even the most energetic

To lay

And dream light thoughts

Of Sunday ice cream

Sweet off your lips

Sunday

She spun and spun

And found herself in capable arms

Much larger than her own

He held her closely

And swore

He would never leave her bedside

After nightly pleasures

And tender touches

Though

His shoes and coat had always

Been set close to the door

He was a charmingly good liar

But

She will never know this

Until many years after...

Sleeping with the enemy

Even lies can be made sweet with just a little bit of sugar.

Sweetener

I was the happiest I had ever been

That's why I loved so hard

Gave you everything I had

But little did I know

My happiness didn't matter to you

Your and my versions of happiness

Were vastly different

Happy

Something about lit candles

And starry nights

Brings the romance out of me

I find myself singing off key

I run food errands way past my curfew

Drive on lightless roads for just a kiss

I find reasons to snuggle

You find reasons to tumble into my arms

Then, the candles burn out

You're nowhere to be found

Memories

PART TWO

FALL

The rain hadn't bothered her too much

That's what she told herself

It softened her skin

Cleaned mud off her boots

Rain watered the dead to green

She appreciated how immune it made her to his bull

For some strange reason

On a particular day

The rain chilled her bones too deeply to stand

Her fingers and toes ached with numbing throbs

She considered finding shelter elsewhere

Or

Permanently forfeiting the prison she called home

For warmer cottages higher in the hills

Escape plan

She had thrown in all that she owned

Her time

Her money

Her weight

Her peace

Her youth

Her patience

When she had nothing else left to give

He felt he had no reason left

To stay

Empty cart

When did *"I love you"* become a chore?

Eyes once you adored

Enrage unjustifiable confrontation

Pillow talk is a thing of the past

Sleepless nights and dark eye circles follow us

Like a daily forecast

I have forgotten the feel of palm lines in casing mine

Lips on knuckles, the caress of wrist and endless time

Now

Days can't go by fast enough

I recite scripted excuses and places to be

Preferring solitude even amongst family and tv

The bedroom is no place to bond and refasten loose stitching

The breeze from an open window is the only calming voice to speak

Giving condolences

Apologies

For not being sound enough to deafen

Nightly arguing

Married

Leaving and coming back means

You weren't strong enough

To go

And will settle

For more years of unhappiness.

Wow

I knew it was over when fall set in

What I thought was ripe and new

The branches drooped

The tithes spoiled always

I had been trained to appreciate

Disappointing taste

Rotting flesh upon my lips

That I never once

Questioned if there was more

Out there for someone like me

I was conditioned

Like my mother

And her mother

And her mother

And her mother

To remain close to dying trees

Expecting them

To bear food for me

To store

Before first snow.

We usually went hungry.

Hungry

It's a mind-altering phenomenon

A split in time and reality

A revelation to stare into a lover's eyes

And not recognize the person

Before you

You feel like an intruder

Has snuck into your home

And refuses to bring back

The man you loved

Burglar

No one ever notices the first shot fired

Until your body aches

Many days after

The initial battle.

You may have won

This fight

But now you live

With a scar.

If the scar is ever retouched or provoked

You explode with rage

As if the battle is happening

All over again.

Old wounds

How many times will you break off a piece of your heart

To mend his missing one?

The real question

Some of us can't stand cold winds

And will cuddle with

A bit of heat

Though this bit of heat

Has a habit of burning you

When you come too close.

Fire will be fire,

Won't it

Body heat

Don't ask clouds to blow

Back from where they came

Fall brought them here

The weather is changing

Seasonal changes

I deserve a round of applause

For caring as much as I did

You were a comedian

I was once your biggest fan

Now

The joke is on you because

I've found better people to love and laugh with

The last laugh

Deep down

You knew he was a project

A build a bear of sorts

Needing thread and stuffing

To fill him out

No woman or father would do it

For some reason

He looks to you to

Patch him up

Dress him head to toe

Teach him the dos and don'ts

On how to be a *man*

The man

He should have

Been made to be

The price was heavy

It cost you your every penny

His heart was last to be bought

Irony

To see him eligible

Tagged for other little girls

With your string and needle

Still in his back

Funny, how he forgets.

Build a Bear

The blind have been known to lead the blind

To dead ins and traps

They don't know where they're going

It's fun to take charge

Even if it risks hurting those

Walking closely behind you

It doesn't matter

Can't care

If you can't see anything

Blind mice

She sneezed. It was a cool November morning.

He hadn't been taught much.

His father wasn't much of much

He could learn from and he'd grown

To make the most of bad occasions

By worsening them with his

Harsh words and violent ways.

November was different,

Because *she was his*

And *he was hers*

A gift, others would have made her out to be.

She was a reminder

Of his failures

Her eyes were a brown smolder

That of her used-up mother.

He didn't have to tell the little girl

This knowledge.

She became aware of it,

Living with a man to monster

Proved her fears right to not

Question father's foresight.

This November was different though,

She required more

To shield the incoming change

Greeting father and daughter at the door

Where he remembered to fasten

The zipper on *his* jacket,

Lace *his* sturdy black work boots

A beanie to redden his ears

He lacked the concern to do the same

For her.

She left home,

Without a scarf to warm her

Heart that day,

And decades after.

Father knows best

Women are no different

You stab her in the heart

With your sharp words

And come back to her

Expecting her to stand

Up straight again

Like nothing ever happened.

Girls are just like you

Carry her gently

She hasn't been

Mishandled

By rough measures

A quick pace

Loosen hands

Eventually fall.

Maybe,

Looking back,

He should have never picked

Her up in the first place.

Vase

When you have to tell yourself

It will get better

There are problems in the relationship

You're avoiding.

Don't lie to yourself

Rebandaging the same cut

Doesn't give the wound enough time

To heal.

Papercut

PART THREE

WINTER

The hardest part is forgiving yourself

For losing yourself

In a relationship

You should

Have never

Been in.

Give yourself time

Sometimes, we learn

More about ourselves

When we are in environments

We don't like

Environments that toughen

Our skin and change the way

We react to petty things.

Sometimes

Don't blame yourself.

You didn't know who he

Really was because

He hid that from

You until he became

Too comfortable

Blame game

You learn to love the person you are when you're all you've got.

A powerful message

You can love again.

But,

It's a choice.

Eventual decisions

I know it was hard

Breaking and tearing everything

You built

Because the foundation

You built you're house upon

Wasn't as sturdy or reliable as you prayed it to be

The good news is

You have the blueprint to design

The home of your dreams and now you see

You've always had the tools to create

It all on your own

Miss independent

Take all the time you need to recover.

In your time

Your life hasn't ended

Your story isn't finished yet

There are still more adventures

Out there waiting for you

To behold love

Just you wait

It had been a cold winter, the coldest she's ever endured. There were times when she thought the rain and snow to bitter and she'd surely freeze from constant winds that hunched her back and inflicted shoulders. She had slaved all her life. Its all she's known, and now that she was free, she didn't know where to go. As much as she cried herself to sleep, surrounded by mountainous snow and thin trees, she saw something. She witnessed the *sun*, for the first time, in years and thought she'd like to see more of it. She packed what little she owned, a coat to warm her faintly beating heart, boots to keep her legs upright, and a scarf made of sad memories and walked away from all she known in quest of feeling the sun's heat once more. She missed the sun very much and wouldn't fold until she bathed in springs light.

The longest winter

You did everything you could

It's not your responsibility to

Drag him back to the safety

You provided him with,

Free of charge

Might I add

If he wants to experience this world without your

Guidance

Let him

You were the best compass he borrowed

If he gets lost, that's on him

Lady map

It's the feeling of

Ribcage breaking

A certain sickness weighing in stomach

That words can't help you to explain

Why you don't

Care to get dressed in the morning

And it pollutes your every thought

You tell yourself, when will it get better?

It did get better.

It got better the second you decided to leave

It did get better

Wolves love wearing sheep's clothing.

A wolf in disguise

One of the best ways to appreciate

Everything you have

Is to lose it all

Thankful

His/her eye wasn't sharp enough

To spot your value

A good eye knows

A real diamond

From a fake one

And he/she treated you like fool's gold

20/20 vision

Free at last, free at last!

Hallelujah!

Crying is good for the soul

Crying replenishes

What's been dry and brittle

Waters seeds that have

Been made dormant

Cleans all dirt and debris

That altered your sight

Now you can see clearly

Tears

In order to move on

You have to forgive everyone

Who hurt you.

If you don't,

You'll end up carrying weights

Too heavy for your heart

Until your back breaks.

Burden

This will be your hardest season

Winter

When you feel the loneliest

You'll remember the good and bad

Memories swirl in your mind over and over again

You might even reconsider going back

Don't.

If being with the one you loved

Left you miserable and hurt

Yelled more than talked

If the romance was truly dead

You've told the same old defeated story

To all your friends and they hate

Where you chose to lie your head

For too many years

Holdfast.

Pray.

But holdfast.

Holdfast

If he wanted to be with you

He wouldn't have made

It hard for you

To love him

It hurts to accept this

Once

Forgive, if you can

Twice

Seems more like a pattern

Three times

It's time to reconsider

Strike

The best way to get out of a pit,

Climb out.

Get to climbing

That relationship did nothing for you

It robbed more than it gave

Bruised when it should have loved

Dumped you in uncomfortable situations

Worshiped the relationship above

Your reasoning

Those red flags went ignored

You told yourself it would get better

But you knew that was a lie

Hid it from your friends and family

Worst of all

You gained nothing worth holding onto

In the end

It tainted your memories too

Honesty hurts

Unhealthy cycles must be broken.

Generational curses

Gather all jagged and broken pieces of your heart.

Set them in cool water

Rinse them soundly

Don't let a single speck of muck remain

Dry them with a soft cloth

Until you can see what your heart used to look like

Before (blank) dropped it

Carefully, glue lines to mesh with others

It will take time for the shape to

Be recognizable

This time,

Don't lend your heart to people

With shaky hands.

Heart surgery

Wolves are attracted to many things

Praying on helpless maidens

Are their favorites

Red Riding Hood

Lessons of the heart are always the worst to learn

But you grow

To be a stronger person

Because of them

Hard knock life

Hearts heal differently

You can't bandage them

Ice won't do the trick

Glue is far too messy

It's not possible to mend a

Heart back together

Because you can't

Reach it.

Time is the best remedy

Time will tell

When you choose yourself

You're making a stand

Defying gravity

Going against the grain

Standing up to those who

Dare strike a fist against you

I feel sorry for whoever

Tries to hurt you again.

Bet

She has been bleeding for a long time now.

Most did not know the cause

Blamed it on unfortunate

Circumstances out of her control

It was not a wound for the eyes

No.

The earth had felt it and so did

The men and women amongst her

She masked with coverup and thick mascara

Wore finely tapered dresses of reds and blues

Her nails were fresh and bright

Not a single hair was misplaced out of style

She made herself appear whole,

And for a time,

Her friends stopped questioning if they should

Tell her the truth,

Though they said it

A hundred times.

She was stubborn.

Afraid, but stubborn

She figured she could keep managing

The pain with cigarettes and being the most

Devoted mother she could be

Her children…

Saw right through her.

They were the only ones

Who truly saw her weep more

Tears to bathe their swollen skin with.

Her hurt, was their hurt

They all wished she could

Wipe the heartache away

Like how he wiped their smiles away

When he,

At five o'clock

Stepped through the front door.

Work hours

You aren't the only one who suffers

In a bad relationship

Family

Friends

Work

Children

Spirit

Most importantly

Your self-esteem

Nobody wins

Why stay in a burning building

If there isn't enough air to breathe with

Fire is constantly burning your skin

Better to jump and deal with life below

Burning building

You were a product of your environment

You weren't raised in a healthy home

Your father wasn't much better

Of course you fell for a man

Much like him

Yes, you survived

Those days are long gone

Battle scars have faded

In the end

It keeps you up at night

When you see what you birthed

Wondering

If they'll be anything like him

Or

If they'll marry him back

Into the family

You've rebuilt

A mother's prayer

Your future is still bright.

Keep this in mind

There's nothing cookies & cream ice cream and a
tear-jerking movie can't soothe.

In bed

Once you get it back

Away from coarse hands

Hold it close to your chest

See and listen to it beat

There's still life inside

Its veins

Your heart will still go on for the best of you

You're still here

After you cry yourself to sleep

Remember

Who made you cry

Promise to swear off men

Who could care a damn less

Pinky swear

Don't tell her to calm down

Can't you see you've put her

Through far too much

She was a rose when you first met her

Not perfect

But she was beautiful

Now you see a petalless rose

Despise the very plant

You tore from root

Because she no longer blossoms

In the matter of your liking

She didn't require much

Sunlight

Proper soil

For you to scan the dirt for pest and weeds

And you failed to do the littlest of that

Before her last petal fell

You cast her down and rode onto the next

Flower to reap

What you didn't know

With sunlight

The proper soil

A good man to scan the dirt for pest and weeds

She was a garden

You are no longer allowed to touch

A new sign sits on her lawn now

Reserved for honest guests.

She is a garden

You deserve a love so deep, water can't fill it to the brim

You deserve a love so grand, masses awe in adoration

You deserve a love so wide, it consumes all corners of your mind

You deserve a love so kind, it bundles you into its arms

You deserve to be loved

What you deserve

PART FOUR

SPRING

You will be someone else's rainbow in their cloud.

Someday

There is a well so deep within you

That none will go

Without thirst

Rubble beneath stones

Will enchant dust

Green and colorful

Bet you didn't know

You could do such wonders

Bet you didn't know

She had come a long way

She met schemers in too vast fields

Where they were bored and she young

She spoke to con men in trees

Their fingers and lies greased to swindle

She sat next to thieves

They tried and tried to take the thing

She loved most

She fought bandits on the road home

There were many

Their ropes were fastened with

Tricks and thorns

All and all

Upon the stones of her resting place

None were able to pry her hands

Open to shatter what she valued most

Her will

Will power

Loving a man made of stone

Thickened your skin

To leather

I guess the positive

The cold doesn't easily

Bother you anymore

Cheap shots

Don't have a chance

Rough and tough

Rise to your feet

Wipe the tears in your

Eyes

Undo your black attire

Remove the sheer veil off your face

Let the sun warm your skin once more

It's not time to mourn

Survivors shouldn't hideaway

In dark rooms

Be bold and face the sky

It wants to greet your

Smile again

It wants to see you run

Survivor

It was never meant to be.

You knew it,

Your friends knew it.

You held too tightly

Onto a thing with loose fingers

And wandering feet.

His eyes always faltered to

Spare change

And you were the million-dollar prize

He was too lazy and immature

To cash out.

Million dollar girl

Set sail and keep from looking back.

There're more adventures for you

Out on blue seas.

Adventurer

Loving a porcupine will ensure a prick

Tempted to hug…

It's better to admire certain creatures from

Afar

Look, but do not touch

He didn't take all you had, you hear me

You're not all washed up

Sentenced to a lonely existence

It's over now

You're free from his hard gaze

You can run as fast as you can

You can be wild and climb trees in your yard

Say hi and bye to whoever you please

Because you are free

You're free!

Freedom comes

Go in and take back the rose garden you planted in his yard

Those are your seeds

He is not permitted to enjoy

The fruits of *your* labor are *yours*

Fruits of your labor

It's a disappointment

When you realize

The sun is brighter somewhere else

And you've been under

Clouds

Cloudy sky

Despite it all

You will learn to be more in love

With the woman in the mirror

Than you have ever before

She won't glance at you in the same fashion

There are scares across her eyes

Bruises on her chest and arms haven't healed

Quite yet

She will be angry with you

At times

Because you left her in unsafe confinements

She did not deserve

She warned you to leave

But you pressed her to stay

Bickering was too loud for her gentle ears

And you told her to mind her business

She cried

You fought her

Until

Until

She broke

She stopped wrestling you

She tired of the battle and turned hallow

Give her time

Tell her she's beautiful again

She hasn't heard it in a long time

Tell her to smile because she has

Much to be grateful for

Tell her to live because she used to live before

Lookup

Clean your bedroom mirror

Once more

Bedroom mirror

Walk like a woman dripping in gold

Pockets flooded with ripe petals

For the occasion

Not a birthday party of balloons and striped presents

Or

A holiday to feast

This is your comeback!

A momentarily tear in your cosmos

The day you slip on $49.99 heels

And strut to songs that flex your calves

From all the whooping and hollering

You're a born dancer

And a damn good one too.

She's a born dancer

A good woman can tell you

She was loyal throughout all his B.S

She shaped him into a better man

But not the better man for her,

Unfortunately.

Sad story

Seasons come and go.

Pray, the bad ones go on a bit more

Quickly.

Seasons come and go

She made it.

To the very top of a hill

She bought

The price was far too

Expensive for her taste

It was durable,

She thought

That was until

Rain came and washed

All grass from root and tree

She stood before a replica

Of a man she once knew.

He was the monster on the mountain all along

Monster of men

Now you know not to be enticed by wolves

With their sweet eyes or soft fur

You came too close

When you least expected it

Fangs bit you hard

Fangs and claws

A bad love taught you what a good love should be like.

A bad love

There will be no more late night phone calls waiting
for you

A quarter past your bedtime

Sleep is a greater friend

He wishes to take you from

This world

To a more peaceful one

Go to bed

Don't act like a victim

Victims wear a defeated mentality

They refuse to move forward

Complaining about the bed they made to lie in

Around the bed, there is a room

Within the room, there is a door

Beyond the door is a world

Get up,

Tuck in your covers and sheets,

Slip on comfortable shoes,

Open the door.

Get up

He's not coming back,

So don't talk about him like

One day he will

It's over

Things ended for a reason

You weren't happy

He wasn't happy

No need to make the past as relevant as the present

He's not coming back

The best way to move forward is to

Take one step in the right direction.

Repeat.

Take one step

That wasn't love.

It wasn't

Love can not only be heard,

Love can be seen.

Amor

I pray for the day when

You no longer remember

All the pain he caused

I can't wait to see you

Enjoying life without him

You'll see or hear something that should

Remind you of him

But it won't

And you'll carry on

With your extraordinary life

An extraordinary life

You can't blame him for your misery

You chose him

You made love with him

You fought with him

You stayed with him

You forgave him

You tolerated his behavior

You continued giving him more second chances

More than he earned

You chose him

It's okay to love someone from afar.

Keyword,

Afar.

Afar

It was on a night like this

She washed off all his memories

From on her skin.

He faintly smelled,

A manly rouge of winter pine

And alabaster soap and mints

So subtle the common nose would not

Distinguish the very fragrance.

It clung to her soul and she cherished

His aroma to where she'd catch herself

Inhaling the good, exhaling the bitter bad

Cause the last of him reeked of smoke and ash

She had been choking on for some time now

Seeking sweeter incense

Her lungs yearned for

She firmly washed

The last of him caked between her palms

The last touch he gave before

He said farewell

Running into another woman's

Breast and arms

Clean, she dried

Swearing to leave what was be

Soap and marmalade

A woman will always have a hard time loving a boy.

Grown woman

I'm not surprised

It did not last

You found him rummaging in the streets

Thinking

In a warm home

Good food

Commodities

Love

He would do good under your roof.

He was wild and untamed.

All he knew was all he knew

He wasn't willing to change

Might have told you otherwise

But he was bound to tar and crumble concrete

And the street lights were a friendly reminder

That he was home and not even

The good Lord could take him

159

From that.

Stray dogs

Never ask a stubborn man to change.

He does what he wants

When he wants

How he wants.

You'll waste your best years

Hoping for anything more.

Your best years

Spring is full of bright new opportunities

The best is coming my love

Waiting for you at a later date

The best to come

Scars teach lessons

The deeper the cut

Stronger the testimony

Testimony

Walking away was the best thing you did.

Good job

Let go of all the heartache

Don't drag your pain into a fresh season

Shred old clothes still embalmed with his scent

Cut or wash or buy new

Burn the dead from sight

Old things are passed away

My mother twisted my unruly locks. Sunday mornings, we had our routines. I'd find my arms upon mother's sturdy lap, her elbows up and rigid. Curly hair was what it is. Only strong hands understand its nature. Mother began with her usual questions and my mindful responses that protected my interest and pride. No woopens today, no nagging needed to straighten my back. She made me listen when I asked her who she loved? *A man of modest approach, his eyes fixed more on her heart than the hips she wore, the red hair sweeping her backside so prized by men like we were the cattle for picking and not the other half they'd been missing. He'll have to love you like how he loves God.* I shook my head, eyes watery cause I'm cursed with a tender scalp. *If he loves God, he'll know how to love you right because God loves him better.*

Mother's lessons

The worst is over

Your journey has just begun

There will be more storms

Of various shapes

Sharing a similar desire

To knock you off your feet

Watching you hurdled over

Is what they hope for best

Be wondrous

A dash of courageous

A pinch of resilient

A heaping handful of confident

The next storm will not know

How to handle a woman

Of your making

The next following round

Storm made

Close your eyes and sleep. Let peace find you in quiet places.

Dreamer

About the author

Ry Reed has been writing poetry for a few years. Poetry has helped her heal and she uses her life as a platform to teach and share lessons she's learned along her journey. Depression, heartbreak, willingness to move forward, and start over again, her poems are relatable, personal, and straight to the point. Her every word digs out emotions and encourages change. She lives in southern California with her mother and brothers and writes poetry, non-fiction, and fiction books.

PINK GRAPEFRUIT

ISBN: 9781797594620

Subjects: Poetry
Visit author website: Ry Reed
Author's Instagram: @ry_reedisme
YouTube: Ry Reed

Summary: Ry Reed's PINK GRAPEFRUIT is her first of many poetry books referencing her life. Powerful, endearing, facing the woman in the mirror, and her broken heart, PINK GRAPEFRUIT takes you on a journey divided between four seasons in her life where love, loss, heartbreak, and recovery are at the root of her poems. Her take on how to move forward is very real and empowering for women still in toxic relationships or survivors.

Latest Releases

THE LITTLE
RED
POETRY
BOOK
CALLED
HEARTBREAK

Grey
STORM CLOUDS

Ry Reed

Ry Reed Books

If you've found this book useful, please leave a review on Amazon or Goodreads and follow me on Facebook Ry Reed poet and author, Instagram @ry_reedisme, or my website Ry Reed's Books to stay updated and catch future releases.

Thank you!

Made in the USA
Coppell, TX
22 February 2021